P9-DNV-718

FRED

The Mouse™

The Adventures Begin

10-15-05
Reese
Haller

Book One

Written by Reese Haller

Illustrated by Lynne Galsterer

PERSONAL POWER PRESS Inc.

Fred The Mouse™
The Adventures Begin

Book One

© 2005 by Reese Haller and Personal Power Press

Library of Congress Catalogue Card Number
2005906390

ISBN 0-9616046-8-9

All rights reserved. No part of this publication may be reproduced, stored in a retrieval system, or transmitted in any form or by any means, electronic mechanical, photocopying, recording or otherwise, without the written permission of the publisher.

Printed in the United States of America

Personal Power Press, Inc.
P.O. Box 547
Merrill, MI 48637

Cover Design
Foster & Foster, Inc.
www.fostercovers.com

Book Design
Connie Thompson, Graphics etcetera
connie2@lighthouse.net

The adventures continue...

The Fred the Mouse series continues with these exciting stories:

Coming Soon...

FRED THE MOUSE   Making Friends - Book Two
Coming Spring 2006

FRED THE MOUSE   Rescuing Freedom - Book Three
Coming Fall 2006

FRED THE MOUSE   School Days - Book Four
Coming Spring 2007

FRED THE MOUSE   Field of Geese - Book Five
Coming Fall 2007

For more information
Visit Reese at
www.reesehaller.com

ACKNOWLEDGMENTS

I would like to thank my dad for inspiring me to write and for telling the Fred story in the car on the way to school. I thank my mom for helping me love to read and showing me how much fun words can be. I thank my brother Parker for helping me remember how the story goes and being quiet while I wrote. I thank Mrs. Galsterer for all the great pictures and for sharing her art studio with me. Chick (Moorman), I appreciate your comments on my word choice and helping me learn more about writing by editing my story. Lastly, I thank my Aunt Jen and Uncle Marty for the financial support that helped me get my first book to print. I appreciate you all.

 # COMMENTS FROM READERS

<u>Young readers have said:</u>

"My mom helped me read about Fred the Mouse. He is a great mouse and I love to sing the song that Fred's dad taught to him. I think Fred has great adventures. I think he will have more great adventures like in his dream at the end."
Mya Watson, 1st grade, Highland West Elementary, Marengo Ohio

"Reese Haller has an awesome imagination! I like how he turned a Tractor into a big green monster, the cool song Fred's dad taught him for safety, and the surprise ending with the crows. If you like adventure and animals, you will love this book."
James Willson Wolfgram-Age 8, Hemmeter Elementary School-3rd Grade, Saginaw, Michigan

"My dad read me the story using different voices. I liked the part about the cat best. It was funny because he lost his lunch. I liked all the pictures too."
Elisabet Barnes, Age 5, Vancouver, Washington

Adults have said:

"The message that Reese has woven into the story of Fred the Mouse will enlighten your entire family, a wonderful tribute to trusting your intuition."
Stephen L. Braveman, M.A., L.M.F.T., D.S.T. Liscensed Marriage and Family Therapist, AASECT Certified Diplomate of Sex Therapy, Monterey, CA

"Reese's book exemplifies the power of family oral storytelling in the literacy development of children. This delightful book can be shared as a read aloud with young children and as an independent reading book for 2nd and 3rd graders."
Kathy Pounders, Teacher, Bay City Public Schools

"Reese has masterfully blended a cute story with drama and suspense. I enjoyed reading the Fred the Mouse story to my daughters using different character voices. We are looking forward to reading the entire series together."
Bryan Barnes, father of two daughters, Vancouver, Washington

"Reese Haller's characters in Fred the Mouse are as genuine and sincere as he is. I'm looking forward to hearing him speak to my third grade class about writing and watching his career as a writer."
Julie Garrison, third grade teacher, Jackson, Michigan, Public Schools

Email Reese with your comments at
reese@reesehaller.com

How it all began

  Many of my friends have asked me where I got the idea for the story of Fred the Mouse. It wasn't really my idea, it was my dad's. When I was in first grade my dad began telling me and my brother, Parker, stories as he drove us to school in the morning. He started out telling us stories about when he was a small boy, or when we were babies. One day Parker asked for a story about an animal. My dad waited for a few minutes and then started telling us about a mouse that lives in our horse barn.

Everyday, we would ask to hear another story about that mouse and everyday our dad would make up another story. I think he would make stuff up that he saw happen at our horse ranch. If it rained or snowed he made that part of the story. If he saw a bird down by the barn, a bird became a new character in the story. Sometimes he would ask us for ideas of new animals for the mouse to meet and what names to give them. We started calling the mouse Fred. My dad told a different Fred story or part of a story every school day when I was in 2nd and 3rd grade.

During the summer before starting 4th grade I decided to start writing down all the stories my dad had been telling us for the past two years. He asked me one day what I thought about making a book about Fred the Mouse. I thought it would be fun to let other kids read about the stories I liked hearing on the way to school. I decided to write a book for young readers so they could learn to like reading as much as I do. And maybe someday they would write a book too.

For more questions and answers visit the **Frequently Asked Questions** section on Reese's Website, go to: www.reesehaller.com

E
N ✛ S
W

Fred
Tricks
CAT

Forest

Big Tree

Fred's burrow
under big rock

Nut
Drop test
of speed

Mr.
Mortensen's
Big Rock

HAWK
ATTACK

FArmer's Field

Mob of crows

Fred's burrow
by corn stalk

CONTENTS

CHAPTER I

The Birth of a Champion

 The snow was piling up outside Arthur's burrow on a late April day. Ordinarily, on a day like this, Arthur would be thinking about the weather. Yet, on this day, Arthur had other thoughts. "Honey, come quickly, it's another one!" The call came from under the corn stalk that Arthur was clinging to. It was his mate, Arlene, a small, light brown field mouse. Arthur, a field mouse with a much darker color to his brown coat and looked like a Baby Ruth chocolate bar, quickly descended the stalk and

crawled into a hole under the roots of what remained of the dried stalk.

"This one is a boy," said Arlene.

"Finally, a boy," Arthur said with excitement, "What should we name him?"

"I don't know. After giving birth to nine girls I have been thinking only of girl names. I was thinking Fredrica until I saw he was a boy," replied Arlene.

"How about we shorten Fredrica to Fred?" suggested Arthur.

"That sounds wonderful. We only have nine more to pick," said Arlene, "but somehow I think that is going to be the least of our problems."

"I know it's going to be difficult to take care of nine girls and one boy, but we can manage it," said Arthur. "I'll help as much as I can."

Fred stared blankly at his nine sisters, yawned and fell asleep. When Fred woke up it was already night and he felt a strange feeling in his tummy. "Come over here Fred dear," said his mother, "and get something to eat." Many of his sisters had already finished gobbling up some of their mother's milk and had fallen back to sleep. Fred wiggled his way closer to his mother and started drinking some of his mother's warm milk. It felt good in his tummy and soon Fred rolled over and fell back to sleep.

Arthur did his best to help Arlene. It

seemed that he spent most of his time gathering food and bringing it back to the burrow.

For the first week Arlene never left the nest. It was hard work keeping all those babies fed. All they seemed to do was eat and sleep. The events went the same for almost two weeks; eat, sleep, eat, sleep, eat sleep. During those weeks Arthur and Arlene picked the names of the girls, a job that was harder than they thought.

At the end of two weeks the children started to dart around the nest and the burrow under the corn stalk began to feel crowded. Arthur decided to give Arlene a break from watching the kids. He announced in a loud voice, "Children let's go outside for some scurrying and scampering lessons. Come along Alyssa, Kayla, Erica, Brittney, Ashley, Hannah, Karla, Rachel, Katie, and Fred."

"Where are we going?" they all shouted at once.

"To the forest and back." said Arthur, "Now watch carefully and do what I do. Scurrying and scampering is a field mouse's most important skill."

Arthur took off down the corn row dart-ing from one side to the other. His children followed him in a line and did exactly what he did every step of the way. When they returned back home Arthur was excited, his children were good scurriers and scamperers. "Good job kids, you all did great!"

Chapter 2

The Big Green Monster

 The first scurrying and scampering lesson went so well that Arthur decided to take the children out into the field one at a time to practice. He quickly discovered who could scurry and scamper the best and who needed more practice.

"Fred, Fred!" shouted Arthur.

"Coming," said Fred.

"It is your turn to scurry across the field

with me," said Arthur, "Remember follow my actions. I made up a little song to help you remember what to do. It goes like this." Arthur started singing in a high voice,

> *First you put your nose up,*
> *Sniff, sniff.*
> *Then you put your ears out,*
> *Twitch, twitch.*
> *Open up your eyes,*
> *Blink, blink.*
> *Then we scurry and scamper.*

Together they sang the song and took off across the field. In no time they were half way to the woods. Arthur stopped and told Fred to continue on all the way to the woods and back by himself. Fred began singing the song and off he ran. Arthur waited and watched closely, the song seemed to help Fred stay focused. Arthur could see that Fred was getting faster.

Fred returned to his father in the middle of the field. He was breathing hard. While Fred caught his breath, Arthur reviewed the safety tips of the song.

"Remember Fred, before you scurry and scamper you must always sniff the air for a fox or cat. You must always listen for a hawk in the air. You must always look for an owl perched on a branch on the edge of the forest. Once it is safe you stay low, and run fast from dirt clump to leaf to rock. Stop at each spot to smell the air, listen for sound, and look into the sky. Always check for safety and then scurry and scamper."

Fred nodded his head as if he understood what his father was telling him and together they scurried and scampered back home.

Fred was so tired that he fell fast asleep as soon as they got home. He had been sleeping only ten minutes when...

R I R R R I R R!!

A loud noise ripped through the burrow. The noise woke everyone up. Arlene and Arthur rushed outside to see what it was.

"Quick, get out! It's the monster!" screamed Arlene.

"Run to the edge of the field!" ordered Arthur.

The children scattered in every direction. The monster was roaring louder now and chewing up the ground. Fred ran as fast as he could, with his father's song racing through his head, and the big green monster hot on his tail. The monster was destroying everything in its path. Fred ran and ran. He reached the edge and looked back to see the monster crush his home and bury it under a pile of dirt. Fred hoped everyone got out safely.

He waited and waited at the edge of the field. "I must be the first one to get here," thought Fred. As he waited he sat and watched the big green monster go back and forth across the field as it destroyed everything. It wasn't until the sun began to set that Fred saw his mother and several of his sisters scurrying along the edge of the field toward him. Fred jumped with excitement. It looked like everyone was safe.

When Arlene arrived at the spot where Fred was waiting she made sure everyone was there. She called out her children's names,

"Alyssa?"   "Here."

"Kayla?"   "Here."

"Karla?"   "Here."

"Hannah?" "Here."

"Brittney?"   "Here."

"Fred?"   "Here."

"Rachel?"   "Here."

"Katie?"   "Here."

"Ashley?"   "Here."

"Erica?"   ....Arlene shouted louder, "ERICA?" Still there was no answer. As she waited, her eyes began to fill with tears. Again she cried out, "ERICA?" This time she heard a voice call back. It was Arthur, "We are over here. She is with me. We'll be right there."

Arthur and Erica appeared over a clump of grass and came running toward the family. They all gathered around and made a big family hug.

Chapter 3

A New Home

 "Fred and I must find a new home. I want you girls to stay here with your mom," announced Arthur.

Fred was surprised. "Me?" questioned Fred.

"Yes, you. You scurry and scamper better than any of your sisters and we need to find a new home fast. It is too dangerous for us to be out in the open like this," said Arthur. Together they both ran towards the woods. As they ran Fred repeated the song his dad taught him. He said it to himself over and over until they reached the edge of the woods.

First you put your nose up,
Sniff, sniff.
Then you put your ears out,
Twitch, twitch.
Open up your eyes,
Blink, blink.
Then we scurry and scamper.

When they arrived at the edge of the woods Arthur stopped to catch his breath but Fred continued on. He scurried through the woods. He scampered by the field's edge. As Fred ran with grace and speed, Arthur watched in amazement. He noticed how fast Fred could run. He seemed to move effortlessly through the grass, around rocks, over sticks, and under brush.

It didn't take long before Arthur heard Fred calling, "Dad I found the perfect spot, come quickly."

As Arthur headed in the direction of Fred's voice he saw Fred standing on a huge rock. "How did you get up there?" he asked.

"I climbed," said Fred.

"But we can't live up there, Fred," replied Arthur.

"No, not up here," shouted Fred, "Under the rock."

"That's a great idea Fred. You go tell the

girls while I start digging tunnels and rooms."

In a flash Fred was off the rock and running down the field's edge towards where his mother and sisters were waiting. That mouse can sure run thought Arthur as he watched Fred scurry and disappear in the tall grass.

"Mom, Mom, I found one, I found one!" shouted Fred. As he came closer his mom and sisters came out from under a large clump of grass. "Come on," shouted Fred. "It's this way."

Fred led his mom and sisters back to the rock where his dad was finishing the final tunnel into their new home. Together the family spent the rest of the night collecting leaves and grass from around the rock and taking it into their rooms under the rock. As the sun began to rise each mouse fell asleep in the soft grass of their new home.

Chapter 4

Seeing, Hearing, and Smelling

 "Fred, Fred, Wake up! It's the first night of our scurrying and scampering lessons!" said Alyssa. As the first born mouse, she acted like she knew everything and was always ordering her siblings around, especially Fred.

"Not until midnight, honey," said Arlene.

Fred inched his way to Arlene and started to slurp his mother's milk. "That is the last time you drink milk," said Arlene. "It is time you all started eating corn."

Arthur passed out a small piece of corn to each of his children. Everyone began nibbling on their piece except Brittney. "I want to drink milk for the rest of my life," she whined.

"I'm sorry dear. You can't." said Arlene in a soft voice. "I don't have any more milk. At least try some corn."

"I don't like corn," protested Brittney.

The other mice sighed and rolled their eyes. Brittney was always whining and protesting. To them she seemed to complain about everything.

"You don't have to eat it if you don't want, but you are going to get hungry tonight at your first scurry and scamper class," replied Arthur. "Maybe you should try some anyway."

The rest of the children had finished their corn and were outside playing tag before Brittney took her first bite. After several bites she joined them behind the rock.

"Okay children it's time for class," called Arlene. "Let's go!" Arlene led the way.

Everyone was excited. "I can't wait to scurry and scamper," said Fred. "I love to scurry and scamper." This was no surprise to everyone else. It was all Fred talked about. Scurry this. Scamper that. Scurry, scamper, scurry, scamper. Fred talked the whole way there.

They arrived at a big rock under a huge

oak tree on the far side of the woods. The limbs of the massive oak stretched up so high and out so far that it created a large open area under the branches. With the protection of the limbs above them, a large group of mice gathered. Most of the mice were children from families like Fred's.

Once everyone was there, an old, gray mouse, using a stick to support himself climbed on top of the rock and started to speak in a low scratchy voice. "I am Mr. Mortensen. I am the principal of this school. Today you begin the most important lessons in the life a mouse. What you will learn in the next three weeks will save your life one day. Learn your lessons well."

Every young mouse stood motionless and did not make a sound. Fred's mind began to fill with questions. "It's just running. What's so important about that? What's all this about save your life? When do we get to scurry and scamper?" His thoughts were cut short by Mr. Mortensen's voice.

Mr. Mortensen continued, "We have created different stations for you. You will be divided into small groups with a grown-up leader. The first station is where you listen to hawk wings and the sound of a cat or fox walking on leaves. At station two we have the smells of a fox, a cat, a hawk, and an owl. The third station will be held out in the field where you will be using your eyes to spot birds in the sky."

Mr. Mortensen called all the children's names and put them in groups of three. Fred was put in Mr. Moner's group with John, a deer mouse with an unusually small tail and Erin, a small field mouse that looked a lot like one of Fred's sisters.

Mr. Moner had a large belly and seemed to waddle like a duck when he walked. He led them to the first station. After listening to the different sounds for about 20 minutes, Fred interrupted, "When do we get to scurry and scamper?" "Later," said Mr. Moner and he led them to the second station. On the way Fred asked, "Do we get to scurry and scamper now?" "No", said Mr. Moner and the group spent 30 minutes smelling fox, and cat, and hawk, and owl scents.

On the way to the third station Fred thought for sure that they would get a chance to scurry and scamper. This station was way out in the middle of a field. But Mr. Moner made them walk in a straight line the whole way. Fred was getting mad. He wanted to run, to scurry, to scamper. As the group sat in the field looking at birds in the sky Fred remembered the song his dad taught him, and he started singing quietly to himself.

First you put your nose up,
Sniff, sniff.
Then you put your ears out,
Twitch, twitch.
Open up your eyes,
Blink, blink.
Then we scurry and scamper.

After singing the song for the third time and staring at the sky Fred jumped to his feet and yelled, "I got it! I know what we are doing."

"Quiet," whispered Mr. Moner, as he smiled and gave Fred a wink.

Later, back at the rock, all the mice were whining and complaining to their parents, "We didn't get to scurry and scamper. All we did was listen, smell, and watch."

Mr. Mortensen interrupted the whining and told everyone to go home and get some good rest. All the mice hustled and bustled, and whined all the way home.

When Fred and sisters returned home

Arlene noticed the sad looks on all her children's faces, except Fred's. She asked, "Fred why are you so happy when everyone else seems sad?"

Fred smiled and said, "It wasn't what I thought. We GOT to listen, smell, and watch." He looked over at his dad and winked.

Chapter 5

Fred Tricks a Cat

 Fred woke-up early the next evening. He was excited. Today would be the day that he finally gets to scurry and scamper, his favorite thing to do.

"Eat quietly, Fred," said Arthur, as he dropped a kernel of corn in front of him. "Your sisters are still sleeping."

Fred was so excited that he took one bite and then ran outside to practice. Fred remembered the lesson from the evening before and how his father's song helped him. He now knew that all scurrying and scampering started with seeing, hearing, and smelling.

Fred knew that he was ready for this evening's lesson. He could feel the energy in his feet. He was ready to run fast. He spotted a leaf on the ground several feet away, he quickly looked, listened, and smelled and then in a flash was off towards the leaf. In seconds Fred ducked under the leaf out of site. He spun around without making the leaf move and repeat- ed the process back to the family rock.

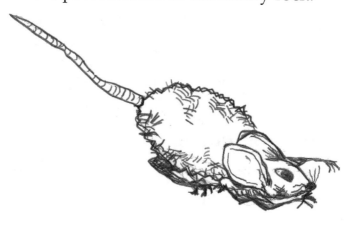

After several trips from the family rock to the leaf and back again, Fred's mom appeared from under the rock followed by his nine sisters. Brittney was whining as usual. "I don't want to go, I'm tired." Alyssa shouted an order to Fred. "Stop messing around, Fred, and get in line." Arlene called out, "Come along, Fred dear." Arthur watched the sky closely for any signs of danger as he followed at the end of the line.

Fred didn't like walking in line so he ran from side to side, pretending to scurry and scamper. When the family got in sight of the big rock where Mr. Mortensen stood, Fred took off running. "That boy sure does like to run," commented Arthur. Arlene called out, "Be careful Fred." It was too late. Fred ran so fast that his mom's words never caught up to him. "He'll be alright Arlene," whispered Arthur. "He's the fastest mouse I have ever seen."

At the rock under the oak tree all the mice from the night before gathered once again. Mr. Mortensen stood upon the rock and announced, "Tonight we will be scurrying and scampering. Find your group and your leader will take you to your lesson spot."

A buzz filled the air as mice ran about bumping into each other and calling out names. It took several minutes for Fred to find John and Erin, the other two mice in his group. Together they found Mr. Moner waiting by the big rock. "Follow me," he said as he led them to the edge of the field. Other groups went into the woods or to different parts of the field.

Before entering the field Mr. Moner stopped and said, "Young mice, we are going to scamper to that big clump of dirt out there in the field." He raised his paw in the direction of a large mound of dirt in the middle of the field. Immediately John and Erin took off running, but Fred did not. Mr. Moner watched closely, but said nothing.

The song his father taught him began to play in Fred's head. He pointed his nose in the air and smelled, He tipped his head from side to side and listened. He blinked his eyes and stared into the sky. When he felt it was safe, off he ran. Mr. Moner could not believe his eyes; Fred was running so fast that he passed John and Erin and reached the clump of dirt first. The three mice waited as Mr. Moner came waddling behind.

"Out here in the field, I want you to practice scurrying and scampering in this pattern," said Mr. Moner, "Dirt clump, dirt clump, dirt clump, leaf. I will be watching

you and giving a report to Mr. Mortensen later tonight. Do that pattern eight times and return to me. Ready? Begin."

Once again, John and Erin took off running immediately while Fred smelled the air, listened closely, and looked into the sky. As Fred ran from dirt clump to dirt clump he sang the scurry and scamper song:

First you put your nose up,
Sniff, sniff.
Then you put your ears out,
Twitch, twitch.
Open up your eyes,
Blink, blink.
Then we scurry and scamper.

The more Fred sang the faster his legs seemed to go. With lightning speed Fred completed the pattern eight times and returned to Mr. Moner first. Mr. Moner said nothing, but Fred was sure he did a good job when Mr. Moner smiled and nodded his head.

When John and Erin returned the group slowly followed Mr. Moner out of the field and into the forest. They walked way into the middle of the woods. It was a lot darker in the woods than in the field. The light of the moon seemed to struggle to shine through the trees.

Mr. Moner stopped by the roots of a large tree. "Line up next to this tree," he began, "From this tree you will now scurry and scamper in a different pattern."

While Mr. Moner was talking the mouths of Fred, Erin, and John fell open. Their eyes bulged. Mr. Moner whirled around and there standing a few feet from him was a huge cat. A small beam of moon light fell on the cat's face, just enough to make its eyes glow green.

The four mice were trapped. Behind them a large tree, in front of them, a large cat. Mr. Moner backed up slowly until he was standing in front of the young mice with his paws spread out.

He whispered, "Stay still. We need a plan."

The four mice stood silent at the bottom of the tree and the cat moved closer.

Fred tapped Mr. Moner on the shoulder. "I have a plan. I will climb up the side of this tree. When the cat looks up, you guys run to that log and hide under it."

"Uh ... okay," said Mr. Moner in disbelief.

Immediately Fred jumped up, grabbed the bark of the tree and started to climb.

The cat's eyes followed him slowly. "Run!" shouted Fred.

John, Erin, and Mr. Moner ran as fast as they could and squeezed under the log. The cat became confused by all the movement and Fred shouting. The cat looked over to find the other three mice gone. At that moment Fred crept around to the back of the tree and quickly scurried down the tree and scrambled under a leaf. The cat looked up. Fred was gone. It walked around the tree and found nothing. After a few minutes of searching the cat realized he had lost his lunch. He turned and slowly walked away.

Fred scampered to the log. "It's safe," yelled Fred. "Come on, let's go home."

Back at the big rock Mr. Moner and Mr. Mortensen held a special meeting with Arthur and Arlene while Fred played tag with his sisters under the tree. Fred didn't know for sure what they were talking about, but he had a feeling it was about the day's adventure and how he had tricked the cat.

Chapter 6

Almost Grabbed
by a ...

Fred woke up the next evening hearing his sisters complaining about having to go to scurry and scamper school again, but Fred was still excited following the adventure with the cat.

"Children, it's time for you to go to school," yelled Arthur from the other room.

Together the family scurried off to school, this time with Fred in the lead. They arrived at the big rock under the tree just in time to hear Mr. Mortensen say, "Tonight is all field scurrying." Fred spotted Erin, John and Mr. Moner. He rushed to them. Mr. Moner saw him coming and said, "We can go to the field now". They scampered off into the field. As they scampered Fred remembered the song his father had taught him and sang it to himself inside his head.

When the four mice got close to the middle of the field, Fred's tummy tightened. He felt like something was about to happen. Not knowing what, he quickly sniffed the air but didn't smell anything different. He listened and heard a strange sound. He looked into the sky and screamed as loud as he could, "LOOK OUT!" Diving straight at Mr. Moner was a hawk. Mice went in all directions. Mr. Moner dove off from the clump of dirt he was standing on and scurried for cover. The hawk reached out with his talons and grabbed the dirt clump that was inches from Mr. Moner's head!

The mice were trapped in the middle of the field with the hawk circling closely overhead. They had only a few dirt clumps to hide under. The hawk dove again crushing another dirt clump in its talons, this time just missing Erin. She ran to Mr. Moner and made herself as small as possible next to him. The hawk circled to make another attack.

Suddenly, a loud noise came from across the field. It was Mr. Mortensen. He was out from under the big tree standing at the edge of the field on another rock. He was yelling, "OVER HERE!" and hitting his walking stick on the top of the rock.

The hawk turned in mid-flight with his eyes on Mr. Mortensen. With a few flaps of his wings the hawk was racing towards the old mouse. But Mr. Mortensen was ready with a plan. As the hawk swooped down, he waited until the last possible moment and then slid down off the rock, out of sight. The hawk missed, this time banging his talons on the hard rock surface. Angry, the hawk quickly turned to attack again, but Mr. Mortensen had slid into a little hole under the back side of the rock.

While the hawk was busy with Mr. Mortensen, Fred, Erin, John and Mr. Moner had just enough time to run out of the field to the safety under the big tree. The hawk flew away with sore talons and an empty stomach.

When the excitement had calmed down Mr. Mortensen and Mr. Moner met with Fred to ask him a few questions about what happened in the field.

"Fred, how did you know a hawk was coming?" asked Mr. Moner.

"My stomach started feeling funny," replied Fred.

"And then what did you do?" asked Mr. Moner.

"I thought I heard something," said Fred quietly.

"What did you hear?" asked Mr. Mortensen

Fred's voice began to crackle, "It sounded like, 'swoooosh' and that's when I saw the hawk coming out of the sky. I didn't know what to do so I yelled."

Mr. Mortensen patted Fred on the head and said, "You did the right thing Fred."

"But what was that feeling in my stomach?" asked Fred.

Mr. Moner looked at Mr. Mortensen, "It's a sense that some mice get when danger is near. It is a special gift that most mice do not have. It has taken some mice a long time to develop this sense. You have it at a very young age. Listen to the feeling and learn to trust what it tells you."

Mr. Mortensen interrupted, "That's enough for tonight. Tomorrow is the final exam. You need your rest, young one."

Later that morning as the sun started coming up, Fred fell asleep thinking about what Mr. Moner said, "Learn to trust what it tells you."

Chapter 7

The Final Exam

 The day started like any other school day, get up early, eat some corn, and head off to school. This day would end different than the rest, but Fred did not suspect anything at this point of the day.

As Fred led his sisters down the path to school, he kept thinking about what Mr. Moner had said the night before. He thought to himself, *What did he mean? How can I trust a feeling? What feeling?*

Fred was thinking so hard that he didn't realize they had arrived at the big tree until he heard Mr. Mortensen's voice.

"Tonight is your final exam. Your skill as a mouse will be tested. Those who do not pass will return for three more weeks of training." Several groans were heard as Mr. Mortensen raised his walking stick and continued, "The test has three parts. The first part is a test of speed, the second part is a test of senses, and the third part is the field test." The young mice stood still afraid to move, not sure what to expect.

A voice called from the other side of the big tree. There stood Mr. Moner with a piece of red cloth in his hands, "Young mice, line-up for your test of speed."

On a tree branch several feet away and

about six feet off the ground stood Ms. Silvia, another teacher at the school. Ms. Silvia stood next to a pile of acorns resting on a bent leaf. Mr. Moner began, "When I call your name step up to the line. I will drop this red cloth and you run to catch an acorn dropped by Ms. Silvia. We'll mark your spot in the dirt if the acorn hits the ground first." Mr. Moner looked down at a long list of names, "Brittney, you're first."

Brittney started to whine, "I don't want to go first. Do I have to, can't someone else go?"

Without a word, Mr. Moner dropped the red cloth and at the same time Ms. Silvia dropped the acorn. Brittney screamed as the acorn hit the ground before she even moved one step. "Go to the back of the line Brittney. I'll give you another chance," said Mr. Moner. "Next ... John," shouted Mr. Moner.

John quickly stepped forward, the red cloth dropped, John took off running and the acorn hit the ground. John's spot was marked about half way to where the nut hit the ground.

Mouse after mouse was called forward, each time the nut hit the ground first and a spot was marked. When it came to Fred's turn every mouse, teacher and student became very quiet. They all knew

Fred was fast, but just how fast was he?

Fred stepped to the line, closed his eyes and took a deep breath. He thought about the cat in the woods and the hawk the night before. His heart started to pound. He opened his eyes, the red cloth dropped and Fred darted off in a flash. He saw the acorn racing towards the ground, He reached out and dove. The acorn hit him right on the head and bounced into his arms. A loud cheer rang out as Fred

caught the acorn before it hit the ground.

Mr. Mortensen was amazed at what he saw. "No mouse has ever caught the acorn before it hit the ground... ever," he said to himself.

When all the mice completed the first part of the exam they all moved to the second phase. For this part of the test each mouse went one at a time into a small hole under a bush. Inside was a large room and another school teacher. In the corner behind her was a pile of different animal parts, a hawk feather, an owl feather, a snake skin, a ball of cat fur, a piece of fox tail. As a mouse entered the room the teacher would wave one of the parts in the air and ask the mouse to quickly describe the smell.

The mice lined up outside the hole and waited for their turn. No one knew what was going to happen. This time Fred went first. He started down the hole, his tummy started to tingle, he stopped, he smelled something, many strange smells came together all at the same time. He immediately turned around and did not enter the room. Seconds later Fred popped out the hole.

Mr. Mortensen could see that something was wrong, Fred should not have returned so soon. "Stop the test," he shouted.

Mr. Mortensen went inside the hole. "What happened," he asked to the teacher inside.

"He never made it into the room. He stopped about half way down the tunnel and turned around. I wasn't able to give him the test," said the teacher.

"Ah," whispered Mr. Mortensen, "Maybe you did. Continue the test with the other mice."

Mr. Mortensen left the hole and called Fred over to the big rock while the other mice continued the test.

"Fred, why did you not go into the room?"

Fred didn't answer. Instead, he hung his head and started to cry.

"Young one, tell me what happened in there," asked Mr. Mortensen softly.

Fred's voice began to crackle, "I don't know, my tummy felt funny and something told not to go any closer. I thought I smelled hawk and then owl, and snake, and fox. I got scared so I just ran out."

Mr. Mortensen looked at Fred with his mouth hanging open, "You smelled all those things?"

"Yes, I think so."

"Good job. You trusted the feel-

ing," said Mr. Mortensen with a smile on his face.

"Did I pass the second test?" asked Fred.

"Oh yes, you passed," replied Mr. Mortensen. "You smelled the scent of danger and trusted your feelings. Running out of that hole before entering the room was a very wise thing to do." He paused and nodded his head slowly. "Come Fred, the others are about finished. It's time for the third phase of the test."

The young mice gathered at the big rock for the third part of their final exam.

"You have one more hour of lessons, one last test. Everyone climb into a cart," boomed Mr. Mortensen.

"Which cart?" asked Hannah.

"Any cart," replied Mr. Mortensen.

All the mice climbed into small carts made out of acorns and tree bark. The acorns helped the carts to slide smoothly over the dirt clumps. The carts were pushed by adult mice into different parts of the field. The young mice were told to wait for the signal and then return to the big rock under the tree. The adults hurried off into the darkness.

After about ten minutes, Mr. Mortensen gave the signal. On the count of three all the adults back at the tree yelled, "GO!"

The young mice began to run, Fred's tummy began to tingle, he stopped and the words of his father's song began to play in his head.

First you put your nose up,
Sniff, sniff.
Then you put your ears out,
Twitch, twitch.
Open up your eyes,
Blink, blink.
Then we scurry and scamper.

Fred's stomach got tighter. He stopped, sniffed, twitched his ears and looked into the sky. The sky was black, darker than ever. He could not see the moon or the clouds and then he heard the beating of wings. The sky was filled with huge black birds. A mob of crows came out of the sky and began snatching the young mice as they ran across the field. Screams echoed through the night. One by one the crows flew off with Fred's classmates in their grasp.

Fred did not run, he made himself as flat as possible and tried to blend in with the dirt. He watched as friend after friend disappeared into the sky. He felt his tummy change, he sniffed, he listened, and he watched the sky. When his tummy told him it was safe, he scurried and scampered from dirt clump to dirt clump. At each dirt clump he took time to sniff, listen, and watch the sky and then scamper to the next clump. Several times birds appeared out of nowhere and Fred would feel his stomach tickle and get tight. Each time Fred found a burst of speed and dodged one bird after another. He finally reached the edge of the field where he disappeared into the tall grass.

In the grass Fred could run without being seen by the crows. With great speed he made his way back toward the big rock under the tree. Fred was surprised when he came out of the tall grass near the tree and saw all his friends gathered around the rock.

Mr. Mortensen standing on top of the rock spotted Fred first and shouted, "There he is. He made it!"

The entire group of mice, teachers, parents, and students all jumped up and began yelling, "Yea Fred! Yea Fred! Yea Fred!" The crowd gathered around Fred chanting.

Fred was confused. "What's going on?"

Mr. Mortensen pushed his way through the crowd and put an arm around Fred,

"You are the only mouse who has ever passed this test in all of mouse history. The crows help us every year during the final exam to pretend to capture the young mice like an owl or hawk might do. No mouse has ever made it back without being captured, until today. You are truly a champion."

John stepped out of the crowd and yelled, "HIP, HIP!"

And the crowd yelled back, "HURRAAAYYY!"

Chapter 8

The Dream

 The final exam was over and the evening began to change into morning. Arthur and Arlene slowly walked the children home. Brittney was complaining about having to go to three more weeks of scurry and scamper school while Alyssa ordered the rest to stay in line. Fred paid little attention to his sisters and walked slowly behind the rest of the family watching the sky turn a pretty orange color.

Back at home Fred felt the excitement of the evening leave his body and he quickly became tired. He went to his room to lie

 down for the day. He slowly drifted off to sleep. Within minutes Fred found himself walking through a beautiful meadow covered with pink flowers with tall green vines. There was a thick fog everywhere, so thick that he could not see very far in front of him.

Fred heard himself ask, *"Where am I? What's happening? Am I awake?"* He felt a weird feeling in his tummy. It was the exact opposite of the one he felt in the field. He did not feel danger. He felt peace.

Fred came upon a building in the middle

of this field. As he rounded the corner of the building he saw a circle of animals. He saw a cat, a dog, a turtle, some birds, and a snake sitting together and talking to one another. As Fred moved closer, the circle opened up and Fred walked into the middle. He felt a calm, comfortable feeling in his tummy. He looked at all the animals and smiled. They all smiled back.

Fred sat up, rubbed his eyes, and looked around. It was a dream, but it felt so real, so peaceful and comfortable. He sat for a long time thinking about the dream and what it really meant. He wondered if there really was a place like that and where this place could be. He sat the rest of the day thinking and day dreaming of such a place.

Fred waited until his parents woke up. Before his sister's got up Fred talked with his mom and dad about his dream. He said, "I am going to go in search of a meadow of pink flowers and tall green vines."

Arlene watched her son scurry along the field's edge towards their old home. She called out, "Be home by sunrise."

Arthur put his arm around Arlene and said, "His adventure is just beginning."

Mice
and others
from

FRED
The Mouse™
The Adventures Begin

ARTHUR: A field mouse with a dark color to his coat and looks much like a Baby Ruth chocolate bar. He is Fred's father.

ARLENE: A small light brown field mouse; the mate of Arthur and the mother of Fred.

FRED: A young field mouse with special skills at scurrying and scampering.

ALYSSA: A field mouse; the first born of Fred's litter; always telling everyone what to do, very bossy.

BRITTNEY: A field mouse; the sister of Fred; a whiner and complainer.

HANNAH: A sister of Fred.

KARLA: A sister of Fred.

KAYLA: A sister of Fred.

RACHEL: A sister of Fred.

KATIE: A sister of Fred.

ASHLEY: A sister of Fred.

ERICA: A sister of Fred.

MR. MORTENSEN: An old gray mouse, the principal of the scurry and scamper school, speaks in a low scratchy voice. He uses a stick to walk and support himself.

MR. MONER: An old deer mouse with a large belly and waddles like a duck when he walks; Fred's scurry and scamper teacher.

MS. SYLVIA: A field mouse and teacher at the scurry and scamper school. She is also the 'nut dropper' for the final exam.

ERIN: A small field mouse that looked a lot like Fred's sister Hannah. She is in Mr. Moner's class with Fred and John.

JOHN: A young deer mouse with an unusually small tail. He is in Mr. Moner's class with Fred and Erin.

Coming Soon!

FRED THE MOUSE™
BOOK TWO

Making Friends

by Reese Haller

Fred stood at the base of a huge pile of rocks. The rocks reached into the sky and seemed to touch the clouds. As Fred squinted to see the top of the pile he pondered a way to reach the peak. A clear path was not easily seen and the rocks appeared sharp and jagged. Fred closed his eyes and listened to his inner thoughts. He took a deep breath and searched for his inner feelings. A tingle started in his tummy and spiraled through his body sending waves of heat to the top of his head and the tip of his tail. What he sensed was not danger or fear but excitement and thrill. Something seemed to be urging him to climb.

Fred opened his eyes and again looked up at the gigantic mound that lay before him. He walked around the base of the pile looking for a place to begin his climb. A rock that looked like the stump of a tree caught his eye. Having scaled a tree to trick a cat when trapped in the woods during scurry and scamper class, Fred decided this would be a perfect spot to begin. He moved up the first few rocks rather easy. His confidence began to build. He jumped from rock to rock and soon found himself half way up the pile. He stopped to look out across the field. He could see further than ever before. His curiosity grew as he wondered what it would be like at the top of the pile.

The rocks were at a much steeper angle on the second half of the pile. The climbing was much more challenging. Fred leaped to reach the bottom edge of a jagged rock and hoisted himself up slowly. His front paws held tight while his back paws searched for a place to grip and support his weight. Fred's right paw slipped and his feet gave way. He hung over the edge dangling by only one paw. Just as his left paw let loose of the rock his feet found a small ridge in the rock and he pushed himself to the next ledge.

The top of this rock was round, smooth and slippery. Fred had difficulty standing on it. To reach the next rock Fred would have to cross a large crack twice the size of his body, and that rock looked just as slippery as the one he was on. A small pebble slid out from under Fred's back foot and fell into the crack. It disappeared into the darkness and Fred never heard it hit the bottom. He looked into the large crack; inside was a vast chamber of darkness. He tipped his head and looked at the rock above him on the other side of the crack. He coiled his body and with all his strength leaped for the rock over head. He caught a small rough edge of the mostly smooth rock and with all his strength hoisted himself on to the rock.

Two rocks to go and Fred would be standing on the top of the pile. Without hesitation Fred jumped to the next rock and quickly onto the top rock. He made it! He stood up on his hind legs in the excitement of his accomplishment and the top rock shifted. He lost his balance and fell to the edge. The huge rock began to slide and then slowly roll from the top position. Fred had to quickly decide to hold on to the rock and possible be crushed as it rolled or to let go and fall out of control. In a split second Fred let go and began to tumble head over tail. He vanished head first into the darkness of the crack he jumped earlier. He bounced off a sharp rock and continued to fall. As he fell all Fred could think of was the hard landing that awaited him. Within seconds Fred hit the ground or what he thought was the ground. His landing was surprisingly soft. Fred sat up and turned to see two yellow eyes glowing at him in the darkness. He froze.

Reese Haller

Portraits by Gregg

Reese is eight years old and a Fourth Grader in Michigan. He began writing short stories in Kindergarten where he was encouraged to take risks with his writing. He discovered his joy and passion in the third grade where he blossomed as a writer.

During the summer before fourth grade, Reese penned the first book in the *Fred The Mouse Series: The Adventures Begin*. For more on how it all began visit the **Frequently Asked Questions** section of Reese's web site at www.reesehaller.com

Reese lives on an Equine Retirement and Rescue Ranch in Michigan with his parents and younger brother, Parker.

Reese's dad is an author of Parenting books and lectures frequently on raising responsible, caring confident children. He also writes a free monthly newsletter for parents and one for teachers. Visit him at www.thomashaller.com

Reese's mom is a Kindergarten Teacher in the public schools where she has taught for over 16 years.

Reese's brother Parker is 5 years old and enjoys rescuing bugs and playing the drums.

About the Illustrator

Portraits by Gregg

Lynne Galsterer is an artist whose creative interests include illustrating, picture and furniture painting, mosaic executing, and home decorating. Although holding a Bachelor of Arts Degree in Medical Record Administration, she has always had a passion for the arts. Throughout the years she has volunteered in various art programs for the Saginaw Township school system. *Fred the Mouse: The Adventures Begin* is the first book she has illustrated.

Lynne was born in Saginaw, Michigan, and currently resides there with her husband, John. She has two daughters, Suzanne and Chelsea, both attending college, and two step-sons, John and Jeff.

Photo by Thomas Haller

 Reese's Charity

I am donating a portion of the proceeds from Fred the Mouse: The Adventures Begin to **Healing Acres Equine Retirement Ranch, Inc.** for the purpose of establishing a reading library at the ranch.

My goal is to create a library and maintain a reading program at **Healing Acres** where children have the opportunity to read with a horse or about a horse while they are visiting the ranch. I envision a place where children can read about how to care for a horse and then have a chance to touch, brush, feed, and even ride a real horse. I chose a wall in the barn that I want to turn into book shelves so people have a variety of reading choices about horses.

As a way to remember their experience I will give to every visitor, young and old, a book about horses to take home.

I want every child to have the opportunity to experience the same joy I experience everyday, the joy of reading and the joy of being with horses.

If you wish to make a donation beyond the purchase of this book, please visit: www.healingacres.com

Thank you for helping me support my dream.

WRITING CHALLENGE

You are invited to participate in a writing challenge. On your own or as a class submit a new ending to *Fred the Mouse: The Adventures Begin.* Re-write Chapter 8 and your ending will be posted for others to read.

Here's how:

1. Read *Fred the Mouse, The Adventures Begin*

2. Invite Reese to your school to discuss the 6 traits of writing or review the 6 traits with your teacher.

3. Brainstorm other possible endings as a class or with your parents.

4. Write a new ending to Book One.

5. Go to www.reesehaller.com and submit your entry electronically. Click the Writing Challenge button in the left column to find the registration form.

6. Visit Reese's site often and read other endings

to *Fred the Mouse, The Adventures Begin.*

7. Be sure to stay true to the characters and the content of the story. Any ending deemed inappropriate by Reese and his editors will not be posted.

8. All submitted material will be sole property of Healing Minds Institute and will not be returned.

PARENT AND TEACHER TRAINING

Portraits by Gregg

Thomas B. Haller, M.Div., LMSW, DST

Thomas currently works in private practice at Shinedling, Shinedling and Haller, P.C., in Bay City, Michigan, as a child, adolescent and couples therapist; a sex therapist; and a chronic pain counselor. He is a certified EEG biofeedback technician, an AASECT certified diplomate of sex therapy, and a certified sports counselor. Thomas has extensive training in psychotherapy with children and couples from the University of Michigan where he received his Master of Social Work degree. He also is an ordained Lutheran minister with a Master of Divinity degree from Concordia Theological Seminary.

Thomas is a widely sought after national and international presenter in the areas of parenting, interpersonal relationships, and chronic pain. He is the co-author of two highly acclaimed books; *"Couple Talk: How to Talk Your Way to a Great Relationship"* and *"The*

Ten Commitments: Parenting with Purpose". He is also the founder and director of Healing Minds Institute, a center devoted to teaching others to focus and enhance the health of the mind, body, and spirit.

Thomas conducts workshops and seminars for churches, school districts, parent groups, and counseling agencies. He is also a regular lecturer at universities across the country.

FOR PARENTS

- The 10 Commitments: Parenting with Purpose
- Raising a Reader
- Raising a Writer
- How to Talk to Your Children About Sex
- Managing Anger and Aggression in Children
- How to Make Your Child Do Homework
  (without having a nervous breakdown yourself)

FOR EDUCATORS

- Transforming Aggression in Children
- Developing Respect and Responsibility in the Classroom
- Bully Proof Your School
- Understanding Asperger's Syndrome

If you would like more information about these programs or would like to discuss a possible training or speaking date, please contact:

Thomas Haller, MDiv, LMSW, DST
Director: Healing Minds Institute, Inc.
5225 Three Mile Road
Bay City, Mi 48706
E-mail: thomas@thomashaller.com
www.thomashaller.com

Order from Personal Power Press

Order toll-free: 1-877-360-1477
Fax (24 hours): 1-989-643-5156
Email: ipp57@aol.com
Mail: **Personal Power Press, P.O. Box 547, Merrill, MI 48637**

Product #	Qty.	Description	Price Each	Total

Subtotal	
Tax MI residents 6%	
Shipping and handling (see chart below)	
TOTAL	

turn page to complete order form

Please add the following shipping & handling charges:
$1-$15.00 . . . .$3.75
$15.01-$30.00 . . . . . .$4.75
$30.01-$50.00 . . . . . .$5.75
$50.01 and up 10% of total order
Canada: 20% of total order. U.S. funds only, please.

Method of Payment

☐ American Express ☐ Discover ☐ VISA
☐ MasterCard ☐ Check/Money Order (payable in U.S. funds)

Card # _ _ _ _ - _ _ _ _ - _ _ _ _ - _ _ _ _

Expiration Date: _____

Daytime Phone: (_____) _____

Signature: _____

Ship To:

Name: _____

Address: _____

City: _____

State: _____ Zip: _____

Email: _____

Daytime Phone: (_____) _____

Nighttime Phone: (_____) _____

School Purchase Orders readily accepted.

Mail to: **PERSONAL POWER PRESS, INC.,**
P.O. Box 547, Merrill, MI 48637
Phone: (877) 360-1477 - Fax: (989) 643-5156 -
Email: IPP57@aol.com
Web Site: www.chickmoorman.com & www.thomashaller.com